Walt Disney Pictures

The Black Cauldron
TARAN FINDS A FRIEND

A GOLDEN BOOK · NEW YORK
Western Publishing Company, Inc., Racine, Wisconsin 53404

Taran was a young pig-keeper who spent his days caring for a pig named Hen Wen. He fed her, bathed her, and played with her.

But Taran did not want to be a pig-keeper. "I should be fighting the Horned King!" he cried. "When will I get my chance?"

"You can have your chance now," said Dallben, Taran's guardian. "The Horned King is looking for Hen Wen. You must protect her."

"Why would anyone want Hen Wen?" Taran asked.

"Hen Wen has magic powers," Dallben said. "The Horned King could use those powers to help his evil cause."

"You must hide Hen Wen in the forest," Dallben
went on. "Guard her there until I come."
"All right. And don't worry, Dallben. I won't fail
you."

Taran and Hen Wen set out for the forest. Along the
way, Taran began to dream of fighting great battles. He
paid no attention to Hen Wen.

When he had fought and won all his pretend battles,
Taran looked down and saw that Hen Wen was gone.

"Hen Wen, where are you?" Taran shouted. He ran into the forest to find the missing pig. "Here's a nice juicy apple for you. Come out, Hen Wen! You know how much you like apples."

A furry creature named Gurgi was living in those woods, and he liked apples, too. When he heard Taran's voice, Gurgi dropped down from a branch. He knocked Taran down, and the apple rolled free. Gurgi leaped after it and picked it up.

"Thank you for nice apple," Gurgi said. "Poor starving Gurgi loves to munch and crunch."

"Give it back!" Taran said. "It's not for you. It's for
my pig. Have you seen her?"

"Piggy?" Gurgi said. "You mean round, fat piggy with
curly tail and big sniffer? I see piggy."

"You saw Hen Wen?" Taran said.

"I see piggy," Gurgi said. "Piggy nice, piggy fat." He
threw the apple core away. "But not see piggy today."

"Why, you lying little thief!" Taran yelled angrily.

Suddenly there was a frightened squeal nearby. "Hen Wen!" Taran cried. He and Gurgi turned and saw a huge bird about to grab Hen Wen in its horrid claws.

"Stop!" Taran shouted as he ran toward the bird. The bird wheeled in the air, and its giant wing pushed Taran to the ground.

"Big bird too big for Gurgi," Gurgi said as he scrambled to hide under a bush.

The bird rose into the air. Holding Hen Wen in its claws, it flew off toward the Horned King's castle.

"Poor Hen Wen," Taran said, looking after the bird. "I was supposed to protect her, and now the Horned King will have her. I must go and save her."

Gurgi came out of his hiding place. "Gurgi come back," he said. "Gurgi want to be friends. Gurgi say don't go to evil castle."

"I must go," Taran said. "Hen Wen needs me. If you really want to be friends, you'll come and help me save her."

Gurgi looked frightened. "No, Gurgi not go," he said. "And if you go, Gurgi never see you again."

"You see," Taran said, "you're not my friend. You're just a coward."

Gurgi watched Taran run off toward the castle. "Gurgi not have friend," he thought sadly. "Gurgi very unhappy."

For the rest of the day, Gurgi wandered around the forest. He kept wondering what was happening to Taran in the castle.

"Gurgi wishes he helped boy," Gurgi thought. "If Gurgi helped boy, boy be Gurgi's friend."

The next morning, Gurgi set out for the Horned
King's castle. He wanted to help Taran. But on the way,
he saw some footprints that looked like pig footprints.

"Maybe boy find piggy in castle," Gurgi thought.
"Maybe boy come back to woods."

Coming around a bend, Gurgi heard music. There was
Taran! With him were a pretty girl and a man playing
the harp.

Gurgi ran up to Taran. "Gurgi so glad to see you! Oh, happy day for Gurgi!"

"Isn't he adorable, Fflewddur," the girl said to the man.

"I don't know, Princess Eilonwy," said Fflewddur. "What do you think he wants?"

"Gurgi worried about friend in castle," Gurgi said.

"You were right to worry," Taran said. "I got Hen Wen out of the castle. But then the guards caught me and threw me into the dungeon. I met Fflewddur and Eilonwy there, and we managed to escape together. But now I can't find Hen Wen."

Gurgi remembered the footprints. "Gurgi see piggy's footprints," he said. "Gurgi no lie."

"You did?" Taran said. "Show us where!"

Gurgi led them to the footprints, and they followed the trail through the forest.

Soon they came to a pool with a path of rocks across it. They started on the path. When they reached the center of the pool, the rocks sank, and the water began to spin. It spun faster and faster. Helpless, the friends tumbled down, down to the underground home of a group of elves called the Fairfolk.

"Hen Wen!" Taran cried, for there was his pig, safe and sound.

"Is this your pig?" asked the Fairfolk king.

"Yes," said Taran. "I'm so glad she's safe. The Horned King captured her, and I helped her get away. But then I didn't know where she'd gone."

"Ah," said the tiny king. "If the Horned King had known your pig was here, he would have tried to capture her again. And if he had found her before you got here, it would have been a bad day for us little creatures. Thank you for coming so quickly."

"Don't thank me," said Taran. "Thank Gurgi. Without him, we might not have found Hen Wen at all."

Taran turned to Gurgi. "Thank you for helping," he said. "You're a true friend."

Gurgi smiled. "You be Gurgi's friend now?" he asked.

"Yes," Taran said, laughing. "I'll be your friend."